FIVE STARS

FIVE STARS

MARION SOMMER

PAPER
WINGS
PRESS

Published by Paper Wings Press.

www.paperwingspress.com

ISBN 978-3-9526009-3-1

PAPER
WINGS
PRESS

The truth is, of course,
that there is no journey.
We are arriving and departing
all at the same time.

David Bowie

FIVE STARS

A Collection of Short Stories

FIVE STARS

Radiant Jewels

Radiant Jewels

Sheyne jumped down the wooden stairs, one hand clutching her comb, the other tightly holding the bar of soap Yovel brought as a gift from his visit to the market in Odessa last week. What a fine soap it was – shimmering softly, looking creamy, and smelling sweetly of lilies of the valley. How exciting that it had been manufactured in a faraway country, France. It must have been truly expensive. She was to be married to young Yovel in late summer. But nobody knew that some days ago, in the darkness of the night, inside the old barn behind the oak trees, they had already come very close to each other. Her face burned at this thought, glowing with boldness and poorly veiled embarrassment.

'Meydele,* don't take too long outside in the garden, will you?' Nerya called out, as she heard Sheyne scurrying through the corridor.

Sheyne rushed past the kitchen and, through the gap of the door, caught a glimpse of her mother's stained apron, as she bent over the table, preparing the next meal.

* Glossary of Yiddish terms on page 13

'Don't you want to take your bath in the lake tomorrow with the other young people?'

'Do not worry, Mama,' she called back over her shoulder as she quickly opened the slanted front door.

At once, a warm wind, scented with the fragrances of herbs and flowers, filled the narrow entrance. With her bare feet, she playfully shooed away some of the chickens jerking their beaks at something on the ground invisible to the human eye. Ambling through the courtyard, she let all her senses seize hold of the midsummer garden flourishing with buzzing insects, birdsong, and flowers in bloom. Sheyne began to gather a few for a wreath but eventually headed towards the outdoor shower, which was set up in a corner of the garden. The screen, made of bleached straw and a wooden frame, was rather heavy as she pulled it closer to the shower – made with a capacious tin can, now filled with fresh, sweet rain water, which could be tilted. From one of the vines clinging to the old fence, she plucked a fat, shiny leaf and placed it on the stump of the old cherry tree for a soap dish. Once hit by a thunderbolt, it now had a niche that offered a perfect aperture for Yovel's soap. She took off her linen nightshirt and carefully hung it over the crooked fence next to the elder bushes that held small ripening berries, just about to change from green to deep purple. Cautiously, she began to tilt the can, letting a small stream of cool water run over her until she could create a mousse of fragrant bubbles, and then slowly work it into her wet hair. She paused the drizzle while producing enough foam to scrub her body from head to toe. Then, she let the remaining water wash it off, as she watched the soapy water disappear between the smooth stones underneath her feet.

'Zeeskyte, please come inside the house now.' Nerya's melodic voice echoed through the garden, hardly drawing her attention.

'I'll be back in a moment, Mama,' she called out at the kitchen window.

By now, she had finished combing her rinsed hair and positioned herself close to the warm screen to let it dry in the friendly rays of the sun. Deep brown, it all flowed down her back and shoulders, flashing shades of auburn here and there. Tiny drops and runnels of water rushed downwards as if in a race, sprinkling the gentle grass, which beckoned her to lay down on its cool carpet covering the earthy hues of garden soil.

She knew well why her mother was nervous about her being alone outside. In the last few days, there had been rumours about a young revolutionary, a goy, a political rebel taking flight and roaming without food, rest, or shelter. Not having understood a word of what was said about him, she now pondered if he would be any different from Yovel. She was not interested in political troubles but certainly cared about exciting stories and young rebels.

Sheyne looked across at the courtyard fence, where the bushes and shrubbery near the beds of cabbages, purple tzibeleh, and strawberries were swaying in a light wind. In an expression of surrender, the fully ripened berries bent their small green necks, carrying their sweet, heavy load and blushing with promises of rare summer desserts topped with sour cream. The warmth and brightness of the sun made her sleepy, and eventually, she closed her eyes right where she stood while the damp dress cooled her body underneath. Slowly but steadily, the enticing scent of the soap faded from her hair. Blinded by the sun, she opened her eyes halfway again. Butterflies were hovering from the mullen to marigold to … and didn't the red berries look like gems shining with an inner light? But wait, there was another, different glow underneath the thicket. Almost like jewels – maybe Sapphire? Sheyne couldn't remember any bluebells growing over there. She decided to maybe pluck some for the kitchen table. How lovely they would look in a vase on the tablecloth …

As she came closer, she saw that those were not flowers, berries, or precious gems at all but eyes. Human eyes that had a passionate look from which light radiated, beaming at her. Being aware that his hiding place had been discovered, a young man emerged cautiously from under the bushes. He looked lonely and a little afraid, and though there was rebellion and courage written on his face, his features were tender, almost feminine. His dirty clothes were ragged, and he was evidently exhausted. Half crouching against the crooked pickets, where, just moments ago, he had been covered by the overhanging lush foliage, he bent his head to avoid the confrontation. Sheyne now stood tall before his hunched body and stared down at him. At first, he did not move, as if frozen, but then, she saw a hand slowly rising towards her. Hesitantly, she bowed down, plucked some of the glowing strawberries, heavy with juice, and then offered one to him. Silently, he opened his cracked lips. He allowed himself to slide to the ground, straightening his bearded chin to look her right in the face. A second berry followed and a third, which he wolfed down, hardly chewing. She rushed to the rain barrel at the corner of the house and filled her small hands, succeeding at saving a few gulps for the fugitive, who was still reaching out for her, almost like a statue expressing a desire that was unknown but strangely evocative. His hand brushed the hem of her simple white dress. Sheyne tried to bring her attention to the muffled sounds coming from inside the house. Then, she lifted her head to take a short but sharp look over the fields of barley and sun-flowers, stretching beyond the fence where three swallows were flicking like rockets. The moment she fell on her knees, her thighs met the hands of desire, whose touch filled her with shudders of fear and longing.

Nerya banged the dough onto the kitchen table with her right hand and began kneading it in circular movements with her left. All her life, she had been teased for being left-handed. Just as her people were harassed now in this country where they had lived for so long. She put the ivory-coloured dough for the challah into a tureen and covered it with a moistened cloth to let it rest while tucking back a few locks of her hair that had come loose in the action. With a tired gaze, she measured the size of the kitchen. How small her world was! The shtetl's tiny houses stood so close to each other. When the winds blew in autumn, the moss growing on the roofs was hurled to the ground in patches, and the smallest of children sometimes ran outside to play with the soft green pads and soiled their hands. No more than three roads crossed the settlement – one leading to the weekly market, where she took small baskets of her berries and some of the eggs that Sheyne gathered every morning. How much better it would have been with a goat, but it was not worth it anymore. After the wedding, they would travel directly to Odessa and stay with Yovel's uncle Baruch, who had only just sold his glass and china trade business.

Together, they, at long last, had decided to do what was unthinkable until then: yetsies. Their tickets for the ship's passage were kept in a safe hiding place inside Baruch's room above his shop, where the new owners were rearranging just about everything. Soon, a suitcase would arrive for her and Sheyne, so she could carefully choose and pack a few clothes and belongings. How all things were beginning to shift! When she was married to Yitzhak, she had worn a veil, and they had looked each other in the face for the first time after the ceremony. Sheyne had known her groom all her life and knew nothing of an arranged marriage, as was the tradition in the past. Her Yitzhak had been so shy! She had liked his face, his soft, sad eyes, and thin cheeks, barely covered with a poorly growing beard. Two years later, he had fallen into the icy river when the old bridge he crossed to collect timber in the woods gave way. He had never learned to swim.

Gazing through the window, she noticed the wind moving the assembly of sunflowers in the fields behind the garden. A sea of yellow and green, lighted up by the sun. The sea, the ocean … she had never seen it before, but soon, she would.

Nerya decided that some strawberries would go well with the blintzes she was going to make for dinner. She took a small basket from a kitchen rack, hurried up to the front door, and then halted. No, better to use the rhubarb stalks she had harvested from their beds early that morning. She went back and fetched them from the cool pantry. While she cut off the hard, inedible parts at the end of the roots, she thought of Sheyne. How engrossed in herself and her youth she was, with its excitements and troubles. Yovel would be a good husband to her. He was a mentsh. So silent and polite. The collars of his shirts always looked clean, and when he played the fiddle, such a kind and calm look spread on his juvenile face. He had seen the ocean many times. Once a week, he would travel with his father, a grain merchant, to Odessa, having business at the Corn Casino. When he was back, he would tell stories about the lovely Alexandrovsky Park where one had a wonderful view of the Black Sea and minstrels sang ditties in the early evening hours. And then, he praised the rich food in the cafés and went on about the bars, cabarets, concert halls, and even a theatre. A frivolous place all in all, where most of the Jewish shop owners opened at Sabbath and where women sold themselves for a few kopecks in the evening. Yovel surely stayed away from all that. Leaving the Corn Casino in the late hours of the afternoon, he would eat kosher meals at some nice place, visit the synagogue, take a stroll in the park, and occasionally purchase a small book or two.

An unusual silence surrounded Nerya. She heard only the chopping sound of her rather blunt knife. Shachar, the knife grinder, had not been feeling well for weeks and was confined to bed. Suddenly, strangely, she felt nourished by the quietness inside the house. Some hours ago, in a commotion, goyim peasants had grabbed their hats from their shelves and left with their dogs to search for a young revolutionary fighter – neyn, a bandit – who was roving around. A nebech in the end. What's the use of being courageous when everyone just wants to stop you? Had he never heard the story of the crabs in the bucket? One crab, in an arduous effort, stubbornly climbs up the bucket wall, and as soon as he reaches the rim, the other crabs pull him back down.

Azoy geyt dos! They would find that schmutzig schlimazl before he created more trouble than they all already had to deal with.

Enough was enough. Nerya put away the knife and briskly walked down the gloomy corridor to tear the front door open. She saw Sheyne with unsteady feet just about to approach the house. Her face was flushed as though she had a fever.

'Meydele, what's the matter with you? Again, you are glowing like an oven!' Nerya touched her daughter's crimson cheeks with the back of her hand dusted with flour.

'Ah, Mama, I fell asleep in the courtyard while drying my hair in the sun. It must have been too strong.'

Nerya grabbed for Sheyne's little warm hand and pulled her inside the stuffy house. 'Genoog! And you don't even know how to brush your hair properly. You are a gornisht helfen! Sit down, and I'll do it for you. And look at your nightdress. It's all damp and crinkled up.' She sighed as she took the comb from her daughter's hand. 'I just ironed it for you yesterday evening! You know how heavy that iron is. This is luxury!'

Sheyne closed her nervously fluttering eyelids, while her mother worked through her long strands of hair to disentangle it.

'And where is that certainly expensive soap that Yovel gave you? That you simply took outside? How do you think I can send you off to married life? Like this?'

All of a sudden, the comb fell to the ground as Nerya abruptly buried her face in her hands. 'Oy vey!' she exclaimed. 'Do you hear the dogs? They must have found him.'

Sheyne's toes tried to bury themselves in the boards of the kitchen floor. She clasped her fingers tightly together and tried to smooth out the folds of her robe as she pressed her hands between her thighs. Then, she realised that she was beginning to faint. As all her senses began to slowly but steadily shut down, there was a single thought repeating in a loop inside her dazed mind: 'If I am going to get pregnant, please let those radiant jewels shine through. Make them appear in the faces of … they will have beautiful faces, this I know … my children. No, my American … grandchildren!'

A moment later, as Nerya peeked through her fingers, she saw Sheyne slide off the chair down to the floor with an unfamiliar and rather rapturous smile on her face.

Glossary of Yiddish terms

azoy geyt dos: that's how it goes
blintzes: thin pancakes rolled around a filling
challah: a special bread of Ashkenazi Jewish origin
genoog: enough
gornisht helfen: good for nothing
goy (pl. goyim): a gentile, a non-Jew
kosher: food that conforms to the Jewish dietary regulations
mentsh: a good person
meydele: girl
nebech: an ineffectual, weak, helpless, or unfortunate person
neyn: no
oy vey: used to express grief, pain, or exasperation
schlimazl: unlucky person
schmutzig: filthy
shtetl: a small town with predominantly Ashkenazi Jewish population
tzibeleh: onion
yetsies: exodus or emigration
zeeskyte: my sweet, sweet one

Mountain Creatures

7

Mountain Creatures

A bald head rose slowly from its desk, which was covered loosely with books – like a pale moon rising above a dark lake in the night, studded with water birds. A pair of Mongolian eyes, set widely apart, impenetrable, and incorruptible, met a walking cane and then the slender figure of an elegantly dressed man leaning on it in a bent posture.

'Have I disturbed you, mein Herr?'

'Uljanov,' said the man as he closed the book in front of him. Reclining back now in his chair, he examined the gentleman's high forehead, eyes that were grotesquely enlarged behind circular glasses, and tiny moustache above his thin lips, which gave away determination and an unerring mind.

'Joyce, mein name. I have a fine collection of walking sticks, mainly to defend myself against dogs, and presently, this rather robust one supports my aching back.'

'The wind passing over the snowy mountains,' Uljanov stated.

'So it must be. What brings you here to these venerable halls of books? Isn't this a grand place?' Joyce made a wide gesture with his free arm while carefully shifting his body weight towards the cane. 'Studies.'

'Of course,' Joyce replied, with a distorted smile that exposed some of the pain in his lower back. 'I came here today for precisely that. Have I not seen you somewhere before? Maybe at Café Odeon?'

'Who has not been seen there?' asked Uljanov dryly.

'Certainly. I will have to sit down though.' Joyce lowered himself stiffly and cautiously into a chair opposite the desk. 'That is the one place in town where important people can be met,' he concluded.

Uljanov began to pile some books and arrange sheets of paper. Outside the high windows, thick clouds were driven by a harsh wind, sometimes giving way to a mellow autumn sun that drew jittery patterns upon the walls.

'Why not prolong the summer days by moving south, like a bird?' asked Uljanov, casting a sharp glance at Joyce's cramped posture. 'There's a place where special treatments are available, unlike anywhere else. You must have heard or rr-r-read about it ... the vegetarian colony Monte Verità and their health retreat programme.'

Joyce couldn't help but smile at the way Uljanov produced the consonant 'r' when he spoke with his bright voice. 'Ah, yes, I have. The mountain of truth. You will never see me there. I heard rumours about patients having to remain without any clothes for hours, even days, exposing their bare bodies to the light and fresh air. It is called, I think, lichtbad ... lichtluftbad. I am not the person for experiments like that.'

Uljanov stood up from his chair. 'In my fatherland, Russia, this would be nothing. In deep winter, people chop round holes in the thick layer of ice on a frozen lake and they dive rr-r-right into the dark, icy water. Naked, of course. It does not weaken them, but makes them strong and rr-robust.'

'That must be so. But you are very different creatures, mind you. The climate in my home country is mild. Mild enough for palm trees and exotic flowers to grow.'

'Then, what is your country, England?'

'Ireland.'

'Isn't Ireland a part of England?'

'Never,' came Joyce's crisp reply.

Uljanov smoothed his goatee and then began to pack a battered brown leather briefcase. His suit seemed clean but rather worn. 'I am no stranger to back problems, whatever the climate. I'm actually interested in these sanatorium treatments. I could spare a couple of days in the coming week. How about you?' He stared at Joyce, who cleared his throat.

'By train?'

'A pleasant journey, not too long, and easily within a day.'

'Well, I have visited the southern part of the country before. Lovely landscape – lakes and mountains. Italian cuisine mostly. Palm trees.'

'Like in your home country,' Uljanov added.

Joyce stiffly lifted himself up from his chair. 'No studies for me today, I'm afraid. The pain has got me tightly in its grip. Additionally, my eyesight isn't too good at the moment.'

Uljanov emerged from behind the desk, revealing a wiry body and well-worn shoes. Joyce shuddered as he sensed extreme intelligence combined with an unwavering will to power. *Precarious combination*, he concluded.

'Meet me Wednesday afternoon next week at the Odeon, and make your decision about Monte Verità. We can both get exposed to sunlight and air – recklessly and shamelessly.'

'Well then, Uljanov. I shall bring my final decision or let my back trouble decide instead.' Joyce laughed uneasily. At that moment, as they shook hands, he noticed that Uljanov's irises were entirely as black as his pupils.

On a cold, drizzly Friday morning, the two men met on the draughty platform of the main station in front of a steaming train.

'Where is your walking cane, Joyce?'

'My umbrella will do.' Pointing to the small suitcase in his other hand, he added, 'I will not need any clothes, will I, Herr Uljanov?'

Uljanov answered with a sinister smile.

Russians are not too conversational when they do not have to be. They tend to be deep thinkers. Joyce tried to soften the onset of panic he felt beginning to expand inside him.

Uljanov, carrying nothing but his battered briefcase, closed his umbrella to help him climb the high iron steps into the vestibule.

I must be out of my mind to go with this man, thought Joyce, shuddering again.

Rain quickly immersed the rattling train in damp greyness as it pulled out of the station. When it emerged from a tunnel halfway through the journey, a different atmosphere unfolded. Here, summer was still in bloom and friendly sunshine floated in the air, illuminating turquoise lakes and the greenery of thick forests.

Uljanov pushed down the window, and a warm breeze entered the compartment. 'See. Little clothing is needed here.' He grinned.

'God save me,' Joyce said to himself. Then, 'Do you believe in god?' he asked, looking at Uljanov who, having pulled out some bread and a large piece of hard cheese from his briefcase, used a sharp-looking knife and offered him a slice.

'God is never on my mind, Herr Joyce. Not even the concept of it. My thinking works on a very different scale. I am too eccentric to give room to any gods. They are all of an inhibiting nature.'

This man even seems to mean what he says, Joyce concluded as he received a substantial piece of cheese that Uljanov had cut off for him and quickly chewed it down. *And must he carry that knife?* He pulled a handkerchief from his jacket's breast pocket and wiped his neck and forehead, finally saying, 'The weather indeed is much warmer here. I can already feel the muscle cramps in my back subsiding.'

'No attempts to escape, Joyce. I have booked our room,' Uljanov replied, with a look as sharp as the knife in his hand.

Joyce responded with a strained smile, 'I have a lovely wife and two lively children who depend on me. This journey reveals my shortcomings in relation to my family responsibilities. You look like a married man too. Where is your wife, Uljanov?'

'At home, Herr Joyce.'

The train entered another tunnel, and Joyce involuntarily turned his head towards the window panel, which only displayed blackness and the reflection of the blade.

'It is the pastry baker who works at the café around the corner. He likes her too much. I believe in the loyal togetherness and equality between husband and wife. Now, with my little trip, she and I are even. You understand, Joyce.'

Joyce sighed, wiped the grease from his fingers into his hand-kerchief, and then folded it back into his breast pocket. 'Now, I am James, Herr Uljanov. I will not stand bare naked next to you and address you as Herr.'

'Vladimir. No vodka here to toast with. But they serve grappa from Italy. We will have it at the station when we arrive.'

'That will hopefully calm my nerves,' Joyce murmured.

Below the train station lay the peaceful expanse of the lake in the warm evening sun, its blue colour almost stinging the eyes. They gulped down a glass of grappa each and then rushed to the rural bus that went to Monte Verità.

'We have to reach before dawn,' said Uljanov. 'The colony is located in a jungle-like overgrown hill, and there is no electricity or even petroleum lamps inside the guest huts.'

'Huts? And a hill? A mountain, I thought.'

'The name is deceiving.'

'So is my self-confidence,' said Joyce to himself, as he clumsily mounted the bus while Uljanov supported his back.

As they walked up to the main entrance of the compound, the sun had set. The lush foliage of huge trees surrounding a gen-erously built villa of exquisite architecture moved slightly in a warm breeze. A few young women, dressed in ankle-length white robes, barefoot, and adorned with wreaths of local wildflowers and leaves in their hair, came walking down a small footpath to welcome the arrivals. Two young men dressed in similar robes with long, uncombed hair and beards joined them. The small group led them up a raw stairway to a modest cottage with the inscription 'Casa dei Russi'.

That should suit Uljanov, thought Joyce, who had abandoned his suitcase to him. *And this is more a jungle than a sanatorium.*

'This is fantastic, Vladimir.'

Uljanov let the suitcase drop on the wooden planks of their single room on the ground floor. Joyce pushed it with one foot underneath his bed.

'Your fears were in vain, Joyce.'

'Please, it's James. You noticed my anguish?'

'There is hardly anything that can be hidden from me, James.'

'Well, I already feel elated. But I'm starved.'

'They'll bring us some supper. It will be frugal though.'

'Frugal? I am as hungry as a lion, Vladimir.'

'It is part of the therapy here.'

With a soft knock on the door, to which Uljanov responded, two young women gracefully entered to place a water carafe and plates loaded with fruits and nuts on the small but beautifully crafted table. A candle was lit. They smiled. Joyce smiled back and spoke a few words with them in Italian. They answered in German. He changed to German.

'You are fluent in all these languages? Your accent seems better than mine. When they hear me speak, they just laugh. Tell them to show me to the bathroom.'

'Fräuleins, bitte zeigen Sie dem Herrn die Erfrischungsräume.'

The fräuleins giggled and gestured for them to follow. The very last light of day illuminated the narrow path leading to another hut, which was almost hidden from view behind dense bushes and an assembly of palm trees.

Singing voices and a gentle knock on the door woke the two men early morning. Joyce, in his pyjamas, pulled away a thin woollen blanket and quickly walked to the door.

'The fräuleins, Vladimir.' He smiled in high spirits as he swung it wide open.

The same two young men appeared in the doorframe. They carried folded robes of white cotton and linen towels. Uljanov sat up.

'Where are the flower girls? And I'm hungry,' said Joyce, revealing a hint of disappointment in his voice.

'This is not a brothel, and you can eat abundantly back home.'

The young men, who obviously wore nothing underneath their gowns, took them to a shed to change into their robes. Joyce and Uljanov looked at each other. Without their customary clothes, their social mannerism seemed to disperse and their individualities somehow surfaced more prominently. Now barefoot, they were guided to a small clearing. Joyce walked up to a large ash tree. Standing close to it and facing it, he eventually took off his garment. Uljanov, next to him, followed and let his fall to the ground. They stood silently. The birds sang. There was distant music hovering over the hill. A slight wind played with the leaves. Joyce began looking up at the crown of the tree. Through the corner of his eyes, he saw that Uljanov's body was as pale as his own.

'What do you do for a living, Joyce?' asked Uljanov sternly, facing the thick stem of the tree.

'I write.'

'Write what?'

'I am a writer. Literature.'

'A penniless craft. Literature has and will never change society and its structures.'

'I agree with you on it being penniless – but not on it having no impact on society. It seems that is what you are interested in. What is your profession then?'

'Lawyer.'

'Lawyers have never had any influence on society.'

'Maybe. Maybe they haven't. But I will. These may be my last days of rest and peace. You will rr-r-remember my words, James.'

Joyce closed his eyes. A sudden sense of tranquillity came over him. Then, he noticed that his stomach was growling with hunger. *I shall walk down to the village below and eat properly*, he promised himself. He began to stroll along the edge of the clearing, taking the shadow line and thinking about how to get rid of Uljanov. Then, he saw one of the young men approach the glade with another visitor: a skinny man in his forties with chiselled facial features, a bronzed complexion, and round glasses in a thin silver frame. He had a rather intellectual appearance. Nodding to the two men, he began to take off his white robe. Joyce nodded back and then walked slowly towards him.

'Good day. Have I seen you somewhere before?'

A lovely and broad smile lit up the face of the new arrival. 'Maybe you have seen my picture in the newspaper. I wrote some articles. But actually, I am a writer who has recently won an award under a pen name. But here … I am only Hermann.'

'So, here we are. Two writers standing naked in this clearing, both wearing round spectacles. And one lawyer over there.' Joyce smiled. 'This is my first day here, and I already feel different, caring less about the world and its narrow-minded human creatures. My back problem, which brought me here, is already ceasing.

But now, I have a stomach problem. If only I were not so hungry.'

'That is always a difficulty for newcomers. They overcome it. And if you don't, you'll find the antidote at a restaurant in the village next to the lake. I myself take refuge there. I am a wine lover.' Hermann rested both his hands on his hips and began bending his upper body to the left and right.

'As am I. Furthermore, I almost faint from hunger. Will you take me there, Hermann? White wine for me only, though.'

'Meet me tonight at the Russian Hut. At nine,' he said in a lowered voice. Joyce looked back at the ash tree, but Uljanov had disappeared.

Hermann, dressed in a linen suit, was leaning against the wall of the Russian Hut when Joyce came out. Without a word, they headed for the main gate and then turned to the road towards the lakeside. They began to walk downhill at a brisk pace.

'There is a lovely old stairway, but it's too dark. No moon to-night,' Hermann said. 'What's your name? First name.'

'James. From Ireland.'

'I'm a frequent guest at Monte Verità. My visits help with my persistent headaches. I do understand your difficulties. But isn't it a delightful place?'

'I'd appreciate it better with a satisfied stomach,' Joyce replied, out of breath.

'We will change that now,' Hermann said. He had a strong German accent.

'Where did you learn to speak English so finely?'

'In India. As you know, it's the national language.'

'You seem to prefer warm climates.'

'I do.' He smiled. 'This place reminds me of India. I would like to live in the area. I am actually looking for a house to purchase close to the colony.'

The lake had appeared within sight with the long row of pretty houses in the front, built tightly next to each other. Entering the promenade, they emerged from the darkness of the slope. Moored boats swayed gently in the harbour. A few people strolled along the waterside under faintly lit lanterns. Hermann scurried into a narrow gap between two buildings, and after a left turn, they stood before an old house with walls made of roughly shaped stones and modest flowerpots on its windowsills. The sounds of laughter and chatter, dishes being moved, and clinking glasses filled the small vestibule. Joyce quickly pulled open the entrance door, and they stepped into a single hall with rows of heavy wooden tables and benches. The place was crammed with guests. Bowls, filled with simple food, and wine crates were everywhere. There was one small breadth of space left amongst the crowd. Joyce followed Hermann and let himself fall on the bench. He felt very happy.

It was past midnight when Joyce slipped quietly into their lodge. During the day, sunrays had warmed the walls and the aromatic scent of timber filled the room. It was pitch black. Joyce groped his way to his narrow bed. There was absolute silence. He found a candle and lit it. He looked at Uljanov's bed. It was empty. With great relief, he changed swiftly into his pyjamas, sank into the thin mattress, and having barely pulled the woollen blanket over his shoulders, fell into a deep sleep. He had never slept with a more satisfied stomach.

The morning knock on the door woke him. He swung himself into a sitting posture with no difficulties. The back trouble was gone. Next, he noticed a black scorpion sitting on top of his blanket. Joyce jumped to his feet in shock and reached out for his robe. The scorpion crawled from the bed along the blanket and down to the floor. Joyce fled the hut barefoot.

Uljanov was walking up and down the sun-lit clearing when Joyce arrived.

'Guten morgen, Herr Joyce. I hope you didn't miss me. I met an old friend and spent the night at that other place.'

'Well, I was just about getting slightly accustomed to your company, Vladimir. But now, there's a black scorpion in our room to also contend with.'

'Do not worry. The species in this region are rather harmless,' Uljanov asserted. 'She will disappear, just as she first appeared.'

Joyce frowned. 'Like each and every one of us, Vladimir. Are they not deadly creatures? And by the way, I was wondering – do you believe there's any form of life after death?'

'Never had time to contemplate that. I am entirely occupied with life and living. Like this, I will get the best rr-r-results of the time given to me here.'

'Not unlike myself, Vladimir. But death … well, is fascinating to me. It can be ugly though and doing its work with cruelty. Nevertheless, I consider it a part of life, not the antagonist.'

Uljanov closed his eyes. 'My brother, who was very close to me, died a very young man. I do miss him. But I never looked into where he might be now. He has since dwelled in my heart. Maybe I continue to live for him, and thus, he lives inside me.'

'What a coincidence. One of my brothers also died when he was young. I named my son after him. They continue living in one way or the other, don't they?' Joyce turned as he heard someone approach from behind. Hermann had entered the clearing and quickly eyed their bare bodies. Joyce then noticed that they appeared as shiny pale as the day before.

'May I introduce … Hermann?' Joyce said. 'Vladimir.'

'Good day, Vladimir. Are you from Russia? People of all kinds of nationalities seem to find their way up here. Not many visitors at the moment, though. It is the end of the summer season.'

'Yes. In fact, we will travel home this very evening,' Uljanov said. 'I have appointments that cannot be delayed.' The bare skin on his head seemed to have in parts taken on freckles.

'Wishing you a pleasant journey then. I will now join the morning dance class.'

'My daughter wants to be a dancer,' Joyce interjected.

'Maybe, one day, she can visit. This place is famous for its professional and innovative dancers. She would surely flourish here.' Hermann smiled at Joyce and then let his robe slide back on his body. 'Good day and goodbye, gentlemen.' He moved away in a slight suggestion of dance and disappeared between the trees. Silence fell on the clearing, and only the birds sang.

Joyce entered their cabin to change into his clothes. He grabbed one of the apples that had been placed on the table and pulled his suitcase out from under his bed. The scorpion resting on it quickly stung his left wrist. An intense pain flooded his body. The door flung open, and Uljanov rushed inside. A woman in a white robe with long blonde, braided hair followed him.

'Vladimir, you cannot go now if this is your last visit,' she whispered.

Joyce sank to the floor. Uljanov looked down at him swiftly. 'What's wrong with you? Have your back complaints flared up again?'

The woman tried to catch hold of Uljanov's arm, who reached out for his old shoes and shabby briefcase. Joyce pointed at the scorpion upon his suitcase, which was quickly disappearing, just as Uljanov had predicted.

'Right, pick up that suitcase. Let's say farewell, James, or we miss the last evening train.'

'Vladimir,' the woman pleaded, while one of the flower girls appeared in the door frame behind her.

Uljanov headed towards the door, and the girls stepped swiftly aside. Joyce followed. Waves of pain moved up and down his left arm. Together they rushed down the footpath and jumped inside the bus that waited in front of Monte Verità. As the doors shut, the two men let themselves fall on the seats, gasping for breath. Joyce looked back as the bus pulled slowly towards the road. The main entrance was deserted, and leaden black clouds overcast the sky. Thunder began to roll in the distance. The rattling bus drove down the serpentine road towards the lakeshore.

Uljanov sighed, pulled out his knife, and began to cut an apple into pieces.

'You know, James, they are potentially deadly animals, but the specimens here don't intend to kill you. And I have the impression that only your left hand is affected. In a few days, all will be forgotten. But you certainly look rr-r-refreshed from our little excursion.'

As Joyce, with a grim smile on his face, bent down to tuck the laces of his shoes, he felt a sudden, distinct pain in his lower back and the sensation of a mild sunburn all over. A cascade of rain started to beat the roof of the bus. In a dim corner by the door of the Russian Hut stood two umbrellas, neatly folded and abandoned, except by a lonely scorpion.

Five Stars

Five Stars

1

Snow fell relentlessly as the train climbed slowly but steadily up the mountain pass. A harsh gale made the snowflakes swirl around in chaotic patterns, while the dark forests, on the slopes, began to vanish from sight under the white load. It was during the second speech at the medical science congress this morning that she realised she was no longer paying any attention.

'Excuse me,' she murmured to the distinguished professor with pale blue eyes and pencil moustache beside her, as she stood up and squeezed past him.

Back in her hotel room, she packed only a few necessities in her travel bag, overcome by that disconcerting beckoning that made her take the next possible train. Now, nestled in a corner of the sparsely occupied, overheated compartment, she kept staring out of the misted window. The landscape at the foot of the rocky mountains rushed past like idyllic paintings of forests, rivers, and lakes being wiped out incessantly by coatings of white. As the train approached the final station, a wide plateau in the high mountains, the clouds dispersed and the sun lit up the expanse of the valley and its surrounding range of summits. It had always been a sunny place. She closed the zipper of her toffee-brown puffer coat, grabbed her gloves and travel bag, and stepped out on the platform. It was modernised, of course but had not been extended in size and therefore seemed smaller than ever. The chill of the high-altitude air made her face tingle instantly, as she headed down the street leading to the town centre. With her boots sinking into the fresh layer of powdery snow, she could feel the older, solid undersurface interspersed with bumpy patches of thick, solid ice. She knew well how to slide and keep on walking without slipping or falling down. There, somewhere on the left, had been her favourite shop, the small town's only bookstore. It was gone.

Flocks of tourists began to pour out of their hotels and guesthouses, clad in neon-coloured sportswear with iridescent snow goggles and carrying their unwieldy skiing equipment and snowboards. Some, in their heavy, grotesquely large ski boots, walked with choppy steps towards the various chairlift and cableway stations. Taking a right turn now, she entered the small alleyway where the tiny record shop used to be. There, as a child, she had bought her very first vinyl record. The grocery store next to it, which was always poorly lit and where she had sometimes flirted with the teenage apprentice, was gone. Naturally, it was now a souvenir shop. The street broadened again, and before long, she caught sight of the hillock on top of which sat the stately hotel. Once, there had been a large meadow right below, all wildflowers and buzzing swarms of insects in the summer. It was kept for harvesting hay by two or three farmers as winter supply for their cattle. It was replaced by a tennis court. She crossed the small bridge over the shallow brook, which was still just the same. Then, she halted and finally dared to lift her head to view the surrounding mountain peaks. She remembered all their names and recalled the various skiing routes she had taken. Hundreds and hundreds of times – no, it must have been thousands of downhill runs.

Taking now to the footpath alongside the little forest, where deer and foxes had sometimes roamed, all too soon, she found herself standing in front of the hotel. The artfully carved wooden balconies adorned its vanilla façade, and behind the high arched windows, she could discern some ruffled, heavy velvet curtains with their pale-rose satin trimmings. Only a few cars were gathered in the front parking lot. It still had gravel instead of a pavement. She chose to avoid the main entrance and climbed up the side staircase to the sun terrace. Several loungers were lined up in a slightly angled row. Plain plastic replaced the once wooden deckchairs with cloths of blue and beige stripes. Nobody was outside.

'Of course,' she concluded to herself, 'people stay away from avoidable sun exposure these days.'

She tightened her grip around the handle of her travel bag and hesitated for a moment. Then, she opened the door that led directly into the lobby and stepped inside. Sunlight flooded the spacious hall with its shiny ivory brocade wallpaper, larch wainscot, marble tables, and coral armchairs with lavish flower arrangements in brass vases in between, giving it all a welcoming and warm appearance. But something was utterly wrong. There was no one around – not a single guest and nobody from the hotel staff. It was absolutely quiet. A slender boy in turquoise knitwear and elegant dark trousers was kneeling on one of the wide, colourful carpets, where he had obviously assembled every single one of his toys: numerous animal figures, small and large houses, trains on their tracks, artificial trees and bushes, action figurines, toy cars, and even a small castle with flags and a draw-bridge. Looking up now, as he smiled at her, he revealed a cute dimple in his left cheek.

'Sorry, ma'am. The hotel is closed.'

He had an endearing face and beautiful light-brown eyes that had a soft sparkle.

'But why?' She gasped. 'It's the height of the holiday season!'

'My parents have just sold it. There's a big farewell party with the staff at Hotel Astoria today. That big hotel next to the lake. Do you know where that is, ma'am?'

'I know. I know where it is. Please don't call me ma'am. I'm Felicity.'

'Fe-li-cit-y!' he repeated deliberately. 'What kind of a name is that?'

'It means the lucky one.'

'And are you? Are you lucky?'

'Sometimes, and sometimes I'm not,' she said.

He stared at her with his mouth slightly open, as if trying to imagine her in both of these conditions.

'What's your name?' she asked to bring him back to their conversation.

'I'm David. But I don't like it.'

'Why?'

'There are too many Davids around already.'

'I like your name,' said Felicity as she took off her faux fur hat. Her white hair flowed around her face and down to her shoulders.

David was quiet for a moment as he glanced at her. 'Whoo! I thought you were much younger.'

'Well, I am. It's just that my hair aged prematurely, meaning it turned grey early. It runs in the family.'

'Why don't you dye it?'

'Oh, my mother did. She used to colour her hair in shades of red, even when she was still young. I never could cope with the odour of chemicals inside the bathroom. So, I decided to do without it.'

'It actually suits you,' he said, tilting his head to one side.

'I think so too,' said Felicity while she unzipped her coat to place it on one of the armchairs. 'But, David, what happened?'

'As I said, my parents sold the hotel. My father's brother died. So, we will take care of my aunt and the three girls. And Dad said this hotel can't put us four children up. We now have another hotel further up on the mountain over here.' He pointed with his finger right outside. 'So, we are going to live there.' He lowered his eyes. 'You know,' he added in a whisper, charged with emotion, 'my uncle died. He died in ...' Then, his voice broke.

'So sorry to hear about that, David. You know, it's all right. You don't have to give me details. I'm sure you'll be wonderful company for the girls. You will help them overcome their loss.'

The boy hung his head and began to push several toy cars towards the castle's drawbridge.

Felicity took a deep breath. 'Sorry that I keep asking. Still, why is this hotel closed in the middle of the season?'

David lifted his head. 'The new owner said he would have the hotel kitchen modernised and some of the smaller rooms converted into suites. He also wants to enlarge the spa area. He said that it was too tiny. Have you come for an overnight stay?' he asked, looking at her small travel bag.

'Maybe, maybe not. I just wanted to visit.' Felicity began to walk around the lobby, as if she were looking for something. Then, she sat down in one of the armchairs. 'David, are you all alone here?'

'The hotel governess is in her room upstairs. She has this thing that women have when they go to the bathroom every ten minutes or so.'

'Cystitis,' contributed Felicity.

'Sorry?'

'Bladder infection.'

'Yes, that one,' confirmed David as he rose from the floor. 'Can I offer you something? Are you hungry? Would you like something to drink? There should still be something in the bar.'

He walked across the room and skipped up the few steps that led to the bar area set on a raised platform. Felicity stared at that space. Then, she saw her father standing there, outrageously good looking, as he, smiling, shook a silver cocktail shaker while sharing a joke with the barkeeper.

'What's wrong, Felicity?' David called down from the bar area.

'I thought, uh, I'd seen ... a ghost.'

'There are surely no ghosts here. I never saw one.'

'You were never scared being here during the off-season with all the hotel rooms empty and nobody around?'

'No.'

'I was. David, you know, a long time ago, my father ... he was once the hotel owner here. That was more than thirty years ago.'

David's eyes widened.

'We sold and left when I was fifteen.'

'Thirty years! My parents are about forty. My family bought the place just a few years ago.' He paused and then said, 'So, you were once the hotel kid here? As I am now?'

'Yes, I was.'

David shook his head in amazement. 'And this is your first visit since you left?'

'It is.'

'This is really cool,' he said. 'How nice you came, while I'm still here. What would you like? Potato crisps? Hot chocolate? But it's only a ready mix.'

'That's fine. Both would be wonderful.'

She glanced down the corridor that led to the main entrance hall, where her mother – a tall, classic beauty always dressed elegantly – had stood often with the guests and engaged in lively conversation for hours.

'You know, David. My parents were both very handsome, even charismatic. I always thought they looked like film stars and should really be on screen – not working so hard in a hotel.'

'What is carry – care-is-matic?' asked David, as he expertly poured the chocolate powder into two large mugs and filled them with the water he had boiled. Felicity noticed that he moved with a confident poise, almost making him look refined – perhaps even aristocratic.

'Well, that's when … when someone is fascinating to other people, sometimes almost magnetic.'

'You're quite striking yourself,' he said.

'Oh, what a gentleman!'

She smiled as she got up and approached the bar to take a seat on one of the barstools. Here, she had sat as a girl, drinking lemonade from a straw while chatting with the barkeeper and his lovely wife, the lissom waitress who always wore an elaborate updo.

David took a closer look at Felicity and noticed the rare green of her narrow eyes, her beautiful lips, and her perfect teeth. Then, he opened a drawer from where he produced sachets with various kinds of crisps and laid them out for her. She chose parsnip and beetroot vinegar. He scattered some into a porcelain bowl and then opened a bag for himself.

'We have green olives marinated with local mountain herbs too.'

Felicity nodded, and then, she turned a little and looked down at the widely spread, picturesque miniature set on the carpet.

'Aren't you a little too old for playing with these toys?'

'Just saying goodbye to them. I'll leave them here for the guest kids. I wanted to see what was in that box with my old toys that I still kept under my bed. I thought it would be nice to lay it all out while being alone here.'

'How gallant of you, David! Maybe you would make a good landscape designer or architect. But I guess you're as good a skier, as I was.'

'You were good at skiing?'

'Oh, I was skiing all the time. Fast, real fast. I liked downhill races.'

'But that's dangerous.'

'It was. I had a few rough accidents, David. On a few occasions, I was hurled up in the air, with and sometimes without my skis, depending on whether the rather simple safety bindings of that time would hold or not. But I never seriously hurt myself. Amazingly, I was always lucky. However, one day, I decided to take the cogwheel railway to the highest summit of the area. It was draped in clouds when I arrived. I was younger than you are now, David. No child ever went up there. I was surprised that none of the few adults inside the cabin or the workers at the summit station stopped me. I had hoped for that. But nobody did. They smiled at me! So, I thought, "No way out now – I have to do the downhill run." It was a somewhat different world up there – so bare. There was nothing but snow and the iciest wind I had ever experienced. The sky was completely overcast with clouds that day, and everything was white – just dazzling white. It took all the strength of my little body and skiing skills to master the slopes back down to the valley below, and they seemed unending. When, after a long time, I finally arrived, I was fully exhausted but very, very proud of myself. The next morning, when I woke up, I was blind. Snowblind.'

'Oh! That was … unlucky!' said David.

'Very! And I had to go to school. It was not that I was completely without vision. I could see contours and contrasts of dark and light but no details. I made it to school somehow. I could only vaguely recognise the other kids and teachers. I found my seat but couldn't read anything written on the blackboard or inside my exercise books. I have not told anyone about this until today – not even my parents. My father would have stopped me from skiing forever, and it was my greatest passion. I kept to my room, and I went to bed early. And I was in agony overthinking if I would ever regain my normal sight. And then, I got lucky again. My eyesight was fully restored after some days. I never went back to that summit.'

David had become quiet and took the spoon out of his mug, which he had kept stirring for a while. 'I'm the first one to hear this?'

'You are, in fact.'

He smiled shyly, then poured a few olives in another bowl, and placed it in front of her. 'I don't ski so much, you know. I prefer skating.'

'Oh, I can imagine you so well on skates. There is some elegance about you.'

Blushing a little, he combed back his dusky blonde hair with his fingers, which had fallen on his forehead.

'There used to be this race once a year,' Felicity continued, 'on that lower hill where everyone – the locals and all the current guests, adults and kids both – could join. It was limited to one hundred participants though. I always went there early to secure my start number. And you know what? Seven years in a row, I won one of the top three positions. One time, it was the first prize. I received a champion's golden trophy! And I was only ten years old. Well, it wasn't real gold though.'

'I've never heard of another kid here like that,' David said. 'That yearly competition is still on.'

'Do you ever go there?'

'Sometimes. But I don't feel like doing it to win a prize.'

'Ah, that's below your dignity.'

'What does dig-nitty mean?'

'That you have earned others' respect and your own just by being who you are. You do not have to make an effort to show that you are worthy and therefore do not feel much need to compete with others.'

David nodded. 'That's true. I don't like competitions. But still, it must be nice to have a shiny trophy in your room.'

Felicity had eaten only a few crisps and now wiped her fingers on a paper napkin. 'Do you happen to stay with your parents in the same extended suite as we did? On the fourth floor to the right?'

'Yes, my room is the one with the balcony and the view of the little forest.'

'Oh, that was mine too! Children always get the smallest rooms, don't they? But then, we grow up and have to walk away.'

They both looked into their empty mugs.

'Would you like another hot chocolate?' he asked.

'No, thanks, David. I have to leave soon. I need to give a talk tomorrow morning at a convention.'

'Would you like to have a look around before you go? Maybe you would like to use the restroom? Or would you like a souvenir from the hotel?'

'That's very kind of you, but no. I guess it's all a bit too overwhelming for me today. And as you know, I don't really like all these empty rooms.'

'So sorry there was no one here today except me.'

'It was my pleasure, David. I will never forget our meeting. I have to try to catch the next train though.'

Felicity slid down from the bar chair, and while putting on her coat, she took one last look around. 'Oh, what I wanted to ask you – is the hotel still rated with five stars?'

'Sure, it is.'

'That's good to know.'

Waving goodbye to David, she stepped out into the terrace.

He followed a little behind her and then waved back. Outside, she put her travel bag down on one of the sunbeds. Here, her mother had sometimes reclined when all the guests had left. She had made a device to get a faster suntan by gluing aluminium foil on a cardboard to place it underneath her chin, something she had read about in a women's magazine. Felicity looked over at the huge birch tree on the little mound in front of her. It was still sitting up there after all these decades. There, in its shade, she had played with her silver poodle, and in the early spring, the mound had been carpeted with deep-blue alpine gentian all over. Now, it was covered by thick layers of snow. Myriads of snow crystals glistened and twinkled as if cherishing her and saying farewell at the same time. She tore herself away from the sight and put on her hat. Looking at her gloves, she became aware that they were of the same colour as those spring flowers. When she walked halfway along the footpath to the small bridge, she heard David running and calling after her. She turned and saw him waving a bag of crisps.

'Fe-li-cee-teee!' His breath steamed out of his mouth as he sprinted as fast as he could.

How sweet of him, she thought.

His hair was flying in the wind, and the powdery snow dashed in all directions from underneath his thick boots. He came up to her, out of breath.

'I thought … you might … still be hungry.' He panted.

'Actually, I am,' she said. 'How kind of you.'

'And I have a … surprise for you!' David was catching his breath. 'A sou … venir.'

'You have? One of your toys? Maybe the drawbridge?'

He brought forth his left hand, which he had been hiding behind his back. 'Look at this!' He gasped.

Felicity's heart took a leap.

'A few days ago … I helped my father clear out some of the reception drawers. We found … a photo album with all the former employees, hotel owners and some of the regular guests. Thinking of your parents – I mean how you described them – I remembered one picture. And I found it again and just took it … out of the album … for you.'

He held it up high for her to see, and they both gazed at the faded colour photograph. 'They really look just like film stars!' he exclaimed. 'Where are they now?'

'Oh, David, they don't live anymore. I have never seen that picture before.'

'They are gone?'

'Yes, they didn't live very long. They had worked much, you know, late into the night, never a weekend off and only two short holidays twice a year during the off-season.'

'I hope you're not running a hotel that way,' he said.

'No, I don't. This photo means so much to me, my little king.' Felicity almost sobbed.

'King?'

'I thought you didn't like your name. So, I made up another one.' She pulled out a handkerchief and cleaned her nose. 'It must be King David, I guess, who you were named after.'

'No, my grandfather was David.'

'Well, to me, you will always be King. You have a somewhat noble soul.'

David smiled cheerfully. 'You can visit our new place next year, if you like. It's Hotel Rose Garden. Dad said that I would take it over one day. The girls don't want it.'

'But then, you'll have to change that name. It doesn't suit you well. Actually, I have something better in mind.'

'Oh, won't you tell me? You must tell me!'

'You know what? You and I – we can play a game. When you figure out the name I have in mind for the hotel, send me a post-card. Here is my address.' She opened her coat a little and pulled a card from the inside pocket.

He exchanged the photo for her card and then studied it. 'Oh, you moved to the warm south. And you are a ped ... a paddy ...'

'Yes, a doctor, a kids' doctor. And you know, I have a daughter about your age. Her name is Rose. Isn't that a coincidence? But, David, you'll only write when you're absolutely certain you have got it right.'

David silently nodded. 'Is there a reward if I get it right?' he added mischievously.

'Sure, there is,' she said. 'You'll get my golden trophy, my one and only championship prize. Would you like that?'

'Felicity ... oh, that would be great!'

She smiled, and they both solemnly shook hands.

The years went by, but a postcard never arrived, and one day, she was certain that her little King had forgotten all about it.

2

Rose walked up to the window, pulled the yellow curtains aside, and opened them wide. A warm breeze entered the chilly room.

'Thanks, dear. I hate air conditioning! It dries up my eyes and throat. Anyway, I could have done without that,' groaned Felicity as she tried to change her position a little.

'Is it very painful?' asked Rose, lovingly stroking her mother's hair.'

'As long as I'm drugged, no.' Felicity smiled, trying not to laugh.

'Will you have to be on a diet without a gall bladder?'

'A little. But there are worse things, Rosie.'

'I have to leave soon to warm up my voice ahead of the afternoon rehearsal, Mum. My keyboardist will bring a few other musicians to join us today. Can I get you something for tomorrow?'

Rose went to the mirror above the sink in the corner of the room. She took out a brush from her bag and fixed her long, lustrous hair. It was still of a rich dark-brown colour with only a few single white hairs. Then, she applied some pink rouge on her cheeks, which just looked great with her jet-black mascara.

'You've got a nice tan these days, Rosie.'

She returned to stroke the back of her mother's hand. 'I've had long walks outside with Tommy … and Robert,' she said dreamily.

'And when will I get to meet the second of these two?'

'Soon!' She laughed and winked.

'And why are you wearing high heels in the middle of the day?'

Rose smiled as she put down a few books on the bedside table. 'You had asked for Voltaire, but I only found some Seneca in your shelves. Will that do? As for my shoes, I'm going out with Robert this evening.'

'Can you sing at all in those things? And they don't really match your floral dress, dear.'

As her daughter bent down to kiss her forehead, Felicity deeply inhaled the scent of coconut oil that she applied during the mid-summer months to moisten her hair.

'I'll perform barefoot, Mum. It's just a rehearsal today.'

After Rose cautiously closed the heavy door behind her, Felicity tried to pick up one of the books next to her but then gave up. She sighed a little and let herself sink deeper into her pillow. Then, she saw that Rose had forgotten her sunglasses. They were still lying at the sink. Moments later, the door was pushed open.

'Ah, she noticed,' mumbled Felicity.

A tall man in a beige linen suit entered the room, holding up a thick bouquet of peonies in front of his face. What was that? Felicity loved peonies. This was Robert, and Rosie had given him a hint! As he approached her bed, he lowered the flowers, showing his eyes. They were behind rimless glasses and had a lovely glimmer. Then, he fully revealed his bearded face and smiled.

'Unlucky phase, is it?' he asked.

'One could say so.' Felicity frowned.

'And who might you be? You are Robert! Or maybe some kid patient of mine? Did I save your life back then? And now, you have come to the understanding that you finally need to thank me?' She smiled.

'May I sit?' he asked, putting down a briefcase.

'Sure,' she said. 'Are you an insurance agent? I'm fully covered. Wait, I'll ring for a vase. No, I can't move. You'll have to get it.'

'I will,' he said and walked out of the room. He came back with the peonies in a vase. Then, he pulled a chair close to her bed. 'Well, you actually did save my life.' He smiled, revealing a dimple in his left cheek.

Felicity grabbed him by the arm. 'David. David, it's you! You're a grown man! How did you find me in this place? I have moved several times since we met. When was that?' Her eyes briefly wandered to the trees outside the window. 'More than eleven years ago?'

He lovingly rested his hand on her. He had good hands.

'Well, Felicity, you know, all these years, I have been writing postcards for you.'

'You have?'

'Quite a few. I always chose the most scenic landscape motifs of the area and the nicest stamps. I wrote with my best handwriting, and I tried to find the right name for the hotel, in different ways. But in the end, I always tore them up. It somehow never felt right. You had no luck with that.' He smiled. 'And my parents ... they knew nothing of your visit. I kept it a secret, our secret. And of course, they always expected me to take over one day. But I had different plans. And then, things turned out in my favour. One of my cousins, after all, did want to run Hotel Rose Garden. And I said, "All right, but under one condition: change the hotel's name." And in that moment, I knew it. I knew the name.'

Felicity glanced at him, mesmerised.

The door opened, and Rose rushed inside.

'I forgot my ...' She halted. 'Oh, Mum, I didn't know you had such a young lover!'

'I told you not to make me laugh.' Felicity gasped. 'Rose, this is David.'

David stared at her, and then, he lowered his eyes and simpered. 'And who is he?'

'That's our secret,' said Felicity.

'My mother is having secrets before me?'

'Every mother does, dear.'

With a helpless expression on her face, Rose fetched her sunglasses. 'Well, have fun, you two. This will accelerate the healing, I reckon.' She smirked a little as she hesitated for a moment and then rushed out.

David looked at Felicity. 'That's how I always imagined your daughter, as stunningly pretty as all her relatives.'

They both smiled.

David cleared his throat and then moved a little forward on his chair. 'Felicity, did you know that there is an old myth behind that hotel's original name?'

'You mean a long-gone dynasty that finally managed to grow a lush rose garden in the harsh climate of high altitude?'

'Not quite. In the Dolomites, there once resided a dwarf king. His name was King Laurin. He lived in an underground palace made of sparkling quartz crystals and had grown a beautiful rose garden among bare rocks in front of its gate. One day, another king wanted to marry off his beautiful daughter, Similde. All local nobles were invited to a celebration, except King Laurin. With the help of his invisibility cloak, he attended the event as an unnoticed guest. The moment he saw Similde, he fell in love, and quickly put her on his horse to gallop away together with her. All knights set out to find them, and soon, they stood before the king's rose garden. King Laurin put on his miracle belt that gave him the strength of twelve men. But seeing that he could not succeed against the knights, he threw on the cloak again that made him invisible and hid in his garden, where he jumped around amongst the roses.'

Felicity's eyes had widened.

'Indeed, those were the long-lost days of magic.' David smiled. 'However, the clever knights shortly detected King Laurin, simply by the movements of the flowers, which gave him away. He was so furious about having been discovered that in the last moment, he turned around to put a curse on the rose garden that had forsaken him – neither by day nor by night should it ever be visible again. But Laurin forgot about the twilight. It so happens that his rose garden is fully in bloom at dusk and dawn, until today. That's how an impressive massif in the Dolomites, called Rose Garden, is lit up in blazing red colours each day.' Then, he added, 'Weather permitting.'

'How fascinating! I never heard of that myth or those mountains.'

'Would you like to see a picture?'

'I do!' said Felicity.

David opened his briefcase and pulled out several sheets of paper, finally producing a picture of an imposing mountain range of bare rocks, probably cut from an illustrated calendar, entirely glowing in shades of pink and red.

'Oh, what colours!'

'This is owed to the mineral dolomite, making the rocks seem glowy when absorbing low sunrays.'

'This is very impressive, David. I'm in awe. But … what happened to the girl in the myth?'

'I don't know,' he said.

Then, he handed her a glossy brochure. A romantic petite hotel sat with a snow-covered roof under a sunny, azure sky. Large blooming roses were painted on its façade. In the foreground, a charming family stood, holding on to their skis and snowboards with beaming faces. Written in golden letters above were the words The Olde King's Hotel.

Felicity was on the verge of tears. 'Oh, David! You got it right. You even improved the name. For me, of course, it was just The King's Hotel. How did we do that?'

'We're a great match, aren't we?' he said. 'But it seems you are quick to cry a little.'

'With you, David. Only with you. Because we grew up in the same hotel. Makes us accomplices, doesn't it?'

'It does, and I'm sorry to find you here in your unlucky state.'

'You know me, I'll get lucky in no time again. But what were you going to do after refusing to take over Hotel Rose Garden?'

'Well, your visit that bright winter's day had quite an impact on me. It was an easy decision for me to become a paediatrician myself, instead of running a hotel.'

'I'm truly amazed,' said Felicity. 'I can imagine how the kids love you.'

The door opened, and an elderly nurse marched inside with firm steps. 'All good with your medication?' She closed the window and curtains, and only then did Felicity notice the instantly missing chirps of the birds outside.

'The assistant doctor will come to see you in a few minutes. Your visitor must be gone by then,' she added as she left, keeping the door wide open.

'I'm leaving in a minute,' David called after her.

They were silent for a moment as Felicity patted her eyes dry, with only the sounds of some people in the corridor filling the room.

'Dear Felicity,' David's soft voice broke in, 'now that I have got the name right, I'm sure you haven't forgotten my reward.'

'No! The gold trophy, certainly. It's yours now. You'll have it as soon as I'm out of here. It's in one of my bookshelves, where it always waited. For you.'

'That is wonderful,' he whispered to her. 'How marvellous that you never forgot. Neither did I. Without fail, the prospect of it kept me invariably in good spirits. Though, to tell the truth, I always considered a postcard too profane. When I finally found the name, I got so excited, because I knew we would meet again. I'm so happy, even if it's under these conditions. But at this very instant, Felicity, I thought of something, well, more … I'd say appropriate … for a prize.'

'Oh my,' she groaned, 'it really hurts when I laugh.'

Then, a little sob followed. 'I know we grew up in the same five-star hotel. Actually a palace, wasn't it? Delicious food in abundance, the best cuisine available. Everything was of the highest standard – the interior fittings and decorations, the highly trained hotel staff, the calibre of guests – all successful businessmen and academics with their families. Even some celebrities came for a stay, and they all loved the small but luxurious spa area. You know, I had access to the key and sometimes swam at night inside the pool in the dark, as if it were mine alone. And you and I – we came to the conclusion that only the best is good enough for us.'

Felicity closed her eyes for a moment.

'Get a pen and paper,' she continued. 'Or for my sake, type it right into your mobile. I'll give you her phone number.'

David softly squeezed her hand a little and displayed a warm smile, the charming dimple deeper than before.

'But you must know there is Robert. And Tommy. It should be really Hunter or Rover – more appropriate for a hound, don't you think?'

A young, balding medic with a notepad tucked under his arm began to enter the room but stopped in his tracks.

'I really don't know if I should laugh or cry now. Where's my hanky?' She let go of David's hand for a moment and rummaged a little around her blanket, while he swiftly rescued the brochure from slipping to the floor.

'Uh, I know what happened to the girl!' she laughed with tears in her eyes. 'But, David, better get out of here before he, over there, in the white coat gets intrigued and begins to examine you. You do appear, after all, like an extreme case displaying excessive patience combined with unusual confidence. Ha, as I had noticed immediately, so calm and elegant, so self-assured, almost royal ... as I said, rightly back then, something like ... a king.'

Akashic Records

Akashic Records

1

'You're late,' he said.

'I know,' she said. 'And I'm sorry. It's too late for that film now, isn't it?'

'Let's take a walk along the riverbank instead.'

'I'll just quickly change my shoes.'

He put on his coat, went down the stairs, and then stood waiting for her in front of the house. Dusk had fallen, and the orange light of the streetlamp opposite was flickering a little. Moths began gathering to dance around its lure. Now and then, small bats circled among the trees of the lane. When she arrived, he rearranged the scarf she had carelessly thrown around her slender neck. She smiled, and they began to walk down the hill towards the river.

'Where's our dog?' he asked.

'We first have to get one,' she said. 'But before that, I must tell you why I was late.'

'Do.'

'I was just about to get on the subway escalator on my way home when I saw my old piano teacher standing in front of that small library on the other side. I recognised her immediately, because she is thin and tall and has these hawk-like features. Unlike what you may think, she always used to be soft and kind.'

'Did you like her piano lessons?'

'In the beginning, I found them fascinating. All those keys bringing about melodies, chords, and rhythm. But soon, I noticed that my fingers were too short to master playing the instrument properly. After some time, I considered myself a failure. My teacher never commented on that. She must have needed the income. My parents were disappointed when I quit. They loved classical music.'

'When was that?'

'Maybe … about twenty years ago? The reason I walked up to her was that she had promised to tell me a story from her life – and only me. But she used to say that I was too young for it. I was quite offended at the time. Holding the proverbial carrot in front of the donkey's nose and not delivering. You start wishing for something you will never get. So, today, I decided that I was mature enough.'

They had arrived at the riverside promenade. The dark water was flowing slowly and silently. Families were out with their dogs – some on a leash, a few of them running free, and some playing exuberantly with each other in small packs.

'So, which dog shall we kidnap?' he asked. 'But it should really be dognapping.'

'Come on … listen to my story!'

He lowered his head and planted a kiss on her forehead.

'Now, hear me out,' she said, as she slipped her cold hand into his. 'At first, she didn't recognise me. But when I explained to her who

I was, she smiled broadly, took me briefly in her arms, and told me that I must hear her story now. She hadn't forgotten. I suggested the library. You know, there are these cosy corners on the second floor where you can talk quietly. As soon as we settled, she said I should listen. Just listen and not ask questions. And that I should put my mind aside. I mean, how can one put one's mind aside? You need your mind to listen, don't you?'

'She probably meant listening without prejudice.'

'Could be. Anyway, it was a moment of suspense, and I didn't care about having a mind or not. She had become older of course but still had that upright posture, even when seated, and those lights shining in her eyes, making her appear like a lighthouse. And then, she began to tell her story. During the early fifties, she was living on her own, giving private lessons in her apartment to students of any age. One day, a handsome student of hers mentioned that he was about to travel to Egypt and was looking for a companion. With her ancestry from Sweden – her name is Anna Carlson – she never meant to travel to an exotic, let alone hot, place in the Far East. What with her fair complexion and all. But it was so that she had a crush on the young man. They chose the best month to travel and planned for a stay of three weeks to make the whole expenditure worthwhile.'

'But how did they finance that? I mean … in those days?'

'He was the favourite son from a wealthy family and, therefore, could ask anything he wished for. Anyway, the day came when they finally arrived in Cairo. After having stowed their luggage in their hotel room and refreshed themselves a little, they immediately wanted to explore the surroundings. Dressed in their light-weight cotton outfits and clutching their hands together, they entered the narrow alleys of the area. And then, something completely odd happened.'

'Street vendors and beggars approached?' he asked, smiling with a glint in his eyes.

'Come on.' She laughed. 'What actually happened was that she suddenly fell into a sort of trance, and when she looked at one small alley, she knew, just knew – "If I now walk down there and turn right, I will stand before that house with the two little balconies at the front." Her companion was taken aback but was somewhat fascinated. So, they entered that passage and turned right, and there was that house with the tiny balconies edged with wrought-iron balustrades. That put them both in shock. But this was not the end. She knew again – "If I pass that building and turn left, I will find that little courtyard with a single tree growing at its centre." '

'And they found exactly that.'

'And they found exactly that,' she said.

They sat down on a bench and stretched their legs. The cool evening wind had settled, and high above their heads, the first evening stars were beginning to twinkle.

'But then, the actual thing began,' she said, wrapping the scarf tighter around herself. 'A few days later, she became quite ill. She ran a high fever – so high that she fainted twice on her way to the bathroom. The young man turned out to be a great companion. She didn't want to see a foreign doctor, so he stayed at her side day and night. Confined to bed, she could hardly move or drink much, let alone eat. The fever was so high that she began to hallucinate. But it wasn't only hallucinations; it was more than that. A door had opened, and she began to see lives ... scenes from people's lives. Maybe her own past lives, maybe others. She didn't know. It was all as if it were on a screen before her. She could barely open her eyes but felt so burdened by the experience that she began to share whatever she saw with her friend, though with difficulty. I can't remember what his name was.'

He took a woollen cap out of his coat pocket to put it on and then polished his misted-up glasses.

'Let's move on,' he said. 'I'm cold.'

'Yeah, let's go back.'

'Do you think that was real?'

'Listen to this now. The young man became intrigued. He was an intellectual and began to prod her, even though she was still running a fever so high that he was considering eventually calling for medical help. Then, he gave her the name of a particular mathematician, Paul Halmos, whom he was acquainted with. Nothing but the name. She played along and began to recount significant milestones in his life. This was someone she hadn't heard of or read about before. He confirmed to her later that it all had been accurate. After that, they stopped, in order to not exert her any further.'

'I like that guy.'

'Anna then told me that she got the upper hand after a few days. She had lost lots of weight and never regained it. She said that when she first looked in the mirror, she saw a ghost in front of her or someone who had visited the underworld. She nearly became afraid of herself.'

He raised one eyebrow a little and suppressed a sigh.

'Amazing, isn't it? Finally, she recovered fully, and once they were back home, her companion wanted to test more of her abilities. They played the same game with some other names, all unknown to her. It always worked. Oh, I took a picture of her today in the library. Would you like to see it?'

'Sure!'

She opened her handbag, pulled out her smartphone, and swiped her fingers across the display. 'Here she is!'

'What an intense glow she has in her eyes! And you're right, there is something bird-like about her, as if she could soar high. Thanks. But what happened next?'

'After a while, she found their sessions too exhausting and decided to end them. But years later, she passed by a bookshop and, recalling Paul Halmos, went inside and found his biography. Browsing through the pages, she saw the details she had divined had been correct, even chronologically. She herself had no idea how that was possible. She wasn't the type to believe in mysticism and never even cast a glance at her horoscope in the newspaper.'

'What a peculiar relationship they shared!'

'Indeed. It seems it was all meant just for that. Anna told me that sometime later, the young man was sent to a university in another city and they didn't stay in contact much longer. They never met again.'

They had arrived in front of the house. He turned the key and, after he took off his coat, put the tea kettle on.

'Have you ever heard of the Akashic records?'

'What records?' she asked as she took two mugs from the cupboard.

'Well, to make a long story short – this is a concept that states whatever has been said, thought, or done … ever is recorded in an invisible universal realm, forever.'

'That's ridiculous. How can that be?'

'Well, that would explain your teacher's initial experience in Cairo and the games of biographical exploration they played.'

'I don't know. Maybe it was all a bit exaggerated. And why, in the first place, would she tell me of all people this story?'

'It must be your exotic looks.'

'You're right! My Peruvian grandmother. I've heard before that I have a slight Egyptian touch. Do we still have some of that vegetable stew?'

'Sure.'

He pulled a large pot from the fridge and placed it on the stove. 'I just recently lectured about Steppenwolf by Hermann Hesse. There is this paragraph where he contemplates the technical function of the radio, which he actually dislikes as a medium for modern mass culture. But then, he expands it further to a symbol for whatever has happened somewhere being available somehow somewhere else. He probably referred to the Akashic records and similar concepts from the Far East. He was fond of India.'

'I can't recall this passage in the book. But if you say so.'

He turned off the stove. 'You're tired, love. Let's lie down for a moment before we eat.'

Taking her gently around her waist, he escorted her into the dark drawing room and let himself fall on the couch, pulling her down on top of him. She laughed when he tried to remove her shirt. Then, his hand touched something cold and hard.

'What's that?'

'Ah, I forgot to tell you. She insisted that I take the bracelet she wore. Anna travelled to India later and purchased it as a souvenir. Pink freshwater pearls and large moonstones set in silver. Isn't it lovely?'

'But you never wear any jewellery.'

'It's beautiful, isn't it?'

She opened the clasp, took it off her wrist, and held it into the tangerine beam of light crossing the room from the streetlamp outside. Then, she tilted it to make all sides sparkle and shine.

'I hope it's a good luck charm.'

'Sure, it is.' She smiled.

Then, he silently took off his clothes and flung a large couch rug over their bodies.

2

'Where have you been? This is my third cappuccino. Ah! You got lost!' She smirked.

'I did.' He sighed and fell into the chair next to her.

'Did you find the old ghetto?'

'No, I never made it there. I got stuck in the mass of tourists. And then, on the way back, I got completely lost.'

He ordered a ristretto and put his camera on the small table.

'But I took refuge in two of those cool, gloomy churches. Not so many people in there. And the paintings and all those artistic decorations … they're awesome. In between, I had some pastry to go. I didn't want to spoil our dinner.'

'Look what I found.' She laughed, pulled a frippery mask out of her bag, and held it playfully in front of her face.

'Very impressive. With those slanted eyes and the colourful glitter, you look like a cat. A cat that wants to go to the carnival, not here, probably in Rio … once in her life.'

'Very funny! You know, I thought we should go to that island over there today.'

'San Giorgio?'

'Is that its name?'

'Another church for me to explore today. Certainly fewer tourists over there, though.'

'But you are aware that we're also tourists, aren't you?'

'I don't really feel like one. It's only all the others, right? I feel at home here.'

'You don't. You got lost!'

Hand in hand, they strolled along the sun-drenched quay, looking for a water bus that would take them to the island. But soon, it was almost impossible to pass through the crowd that was moving in chaotic patterns between the kiosks ridiculously loaded with cheap souvenirs, certainly manufactured in faraway countries.

'Let's take that vaporetto over here,' he said. 'By the way, did you know that the smaller canals are actually called rio and that they are crossed by more than 400 bridges?'

'Good that you counted them for me today. I was too lazy to do that.' She smiled.

'Oh! They are just about to take off,' he called, 'but we must scan our tickets first!'

They rushed onto the floating platform, where the water bus had been moored by ropes, and he stepped on board. When he looked back, she had disappeared. Then, he saw her red dress flowing around her slender body as she ran back to the quay. Fear gripped his heart as the boat pulled off into the unsettled waters of the lagoon. He called her name. She turned around, and through the roar of the motors, he heard her shout something about her bracelet and saw her gesturing that she would take the next water bus. She became smaller and smaller as the boat speeded up, and she hurried away in the other direction. Then, she disappeared into the throng.

With a feeling of trepidation in his stomach, he stepped inside the damp interior of the packed vaporetto and let himself sink onto one of the hard plastic seats. Looking outside through the smeared window panels, the thought suddenly crossed his mind that she had always been an apparition and that he might never see her again. San Giorgio was becoming larger and the view back to San Marco increasingly enchanting. Maybe this was all but a mirage and she also had always been only that. He looked around to see if he could find some familiar faces, but there were none. In the last two days, he had squeezed himself past so many tourists, sometimes stumbling into those who wouldn't move on. There seemed to be an endless supply of them, and one never met the same people anywhere.

At San Giorgio, he left the watercraft and its incessant rocking, which had added to his unease. With the relief of standing on solid ground, he looked up at the soaring bell tower of the church in front of him. Then, he turned and gazed back across the aquamarine expanse of water to the main island in the distance. He tried to spot a red dress. There were none. Or many. From the distance, it had all become one single conglomeration of grey.

He strolled up and down the small pier. If he went back now, their water buses might simply cross each other. He couldn't even remember whether she had worn her bracelet today or not. People began to gather on the landing stage for the next boat. He noticed a man standing near the waterfront, tall and thin with grey hair, a sunburnt complexion, and piercing eyes. He had a distinctive profile and kept looking at his watch. Shaking off the numbness and fear that engulfed him, he approached the elderly gentleman.

'Hello, it's quite a view, isn't it?'

'Indeed. Nothing missing. Pure perfection.'

'May I ask you … I'm a bit thirsty. Would you like to join me for a drink in the little bistro behind us?'

The grey-bearded man turned and inspected him sharply. Then, he laughed and said he usually wouldn't do things like that, especially on the day of his departure. But he felt like making an exception and would certainly enjoy some refreshment. He had only half an hour to spare though.

They ordered sparkling water and salted pistachios. Then, they discussed the local food … at some places, delicious, while in others, well … haha! They enthused over the play of light reflecting on the water and the façades of the palaces lining the Canal Grande, ever-changing each moment of the day. Then, that in the early morning and late evenings, Venice was almost deserted. But why? They endeavoured to bring up writers who had lived or were buried there, even daughters of writers, and went on to discuss the kitsch that had become so prominent in the shops.

The man looked at his watch, smiled, stood up, and said that he had to leave, that he didn't want to, but then the flight he had booked would be missing one passenger … haha!

Hastily, they walked back to the pier, boarded the waiting vaporetto, and sitting next to each other, watched the tower of San Giorgio becoming smaller.

'May I ask you something?'

'You're welcome to. Our little rest invigorated me. Thank you for that.'

'Are you – is your family originally from a Scandinavian country?'

'Ah, I know. You're asking because of my sunburnt face. My parents were half Swedish, half Polish. But Denmark is where I grew up.'

'Your name would not be Carlson by chance?'

'No, sorry, it's Erikson.' He smiled and looked at his watch.

The winged Lion of Venice, towering on his column before the Piazza San Marco, came into view and grew larger while people began to get up and surge towards the boat's exit.

'My sister was a Carlson, after her marriage. But it's a very common name.'

'Was she Anna?'

'Annika. Annika Carlson. A teacher of classical piano.'

'I can't believe this.'

'Why? Do you know someone by the same name?' The old man stood up. 'Unfortunately, my sister died a few months ago.'

'She died? This is all unbelievable. My wife was one of her students when she was little. They accidentally met only last year, and she told me some interesting things about your sister.'

'That is more than impressive. How small this world is! But actually, all the world gathers here, doesn't it?'

They were pushed onto the quay by the other passengers streaming out of the vehicle. Then, they halted for a moment and looked up at the sun-lit Palazzo Ducale and then at each other.

'What a pity I have to leave. I really have to hurry up. Please give my regards to your wife. What a remarkable meeting! Is she also here?'

'Yes, she must be somewhere. Really, in fact, she is just now looking for …'

'So sorry, but I have to go. All the best to you both.'

They shook hands with smiles, and then, the old man turned and disappeared into the crowd.

. . .

'You're late,' she said. 'This is my second gelato.'

Then, she lifted her right arm high up in the air and pulled back the sleeve of her dress. The bracelet glistened and twinkled in the last rays of sun that were painting the piazza in warm orange hues.

'Where was it?'

'I never wore it today. I had left it in the hotel, in the drawer of my bedside table. How was San Giorgio?'

'I didn't see much of it. I missed you.'

She took off her sunglasses and smiled at him. 'Shall we eat here properly? I'm hungry.'

'I'd actually like to stroll around the piazza a little. Look at this sunset! Are there now more doves around than during the day or fewer? And I must tell you who I just met.'

'Death in Venice?' She laughed.

'How do you know that?'

'Why not take a real holiday and not think of books for a while?'

'It was you who just mentioned it. And you won't buy that now. At San Giorgio, I met a relative of your piano teacher. And not just anyone. It was her brother.'

Her lips curved to say 'Wha –', and then, she blurted, 'How is that possible? This is unbelievable. How did you find out?'

'Well, he looked just like her.'

'And all the while I was searching for her bracelet? Unbeliev-able.' She gasped, shook her head, and laughed. 'How was he?'

'A kind, well-groomed elderly gentleman. We didn't have much time though.'

'Where is he now? I would like to meet him.'

'Sadly, he had to leave today.'

'Oh,' she said. 'But where is death in that? Did he look that old, or was he not well?'

'He told me that his sister had died, just recently.'

'What?'

'And did you know that she was half Polish? He couldn't tell me more. He had to catch his flight.'

'Oh, I would have loved to meet him!'

As they strolled towards the restaurant, they found the tall, wrought-iron black posts with their pink lanterns now lit up, and the live orchestras had begun to play their tunes, resonating over the piazza. When they were back, all the tables had already been taken.

'You know, all this wouldn't have happened the way it did if we had not decided to leave our phones today for once. I wouldn't have noticed Anna's brother standing there. I would have been talking to you on the phone instead.'

'Maybe we can do this more often. Shall we eat at the restaurant in our hotel? Shall we take one of those gondolas over there?'

After having taken their seats, the gondolier began quickly to steer the black lacquered boat into smaller canals, and all was silent and peaceful. He buried his face into her hair, which was flowing down her shoulders, and whispered, 'But, you know, something inside me also died today. That old inattentive fellow who, instead of admiring his wife every day, doesn't really look at her and is unaware whether she's wearing her bracelet or not. And who's instead happy that she's there and not only a figment made up in his mind.'

She blushed and whispered back into his ear, 'And now, let's hope the gondolier didn't understand a word of that.'

The Dull Sea Mare

The Dull Sea Mare

CACOPHONOUS SOUNDS

Clara weighed the packet in her arms. It was heavier than she had expected it to be. The appointment was later in the afternoon, but she had begun to hurry up. By now, the traffic had thickened and the blazing sun nearly melted the pavement she scurried along. Only a short while earlier, she kept walking right alongside the shopfronts to avoid bumping into people unnecessarily. When, now and then, the glass panes reflected the glaring rays, it was like being braced by twin suns. Then, suddenly, she saw it. Almost while passing by a window displaying antiques from possibly all decades and centuries gone by, she saw it lying there, in a dismal niche. She recognised it within a second – a dulcimer. The musical instrument she had always wanted to play. Upon its fading varnish idled a few specks of sunlight that had made their way into the dingy shop's interior. The darkened and rusty strings looked lifeless, but once they were replaced, they would be as good as new.

Little bells were set dutifully in motion when she pushed the door open to step inside. A large fan rotating high above was tiredly shuffling stale air. There was silence; dust particles floated about calmly, while a confusing amount of furniture of various shapes and sizes provided only narrow aisles to move around the store. Painted porcelain figurines and vintage dolls, sets of floral dishes, bulky tea pots, silver cutlery, rhinestone table lamps, dulled jewellery, and dark oil paintings had been placed on every available surface. Clara stumbled over thick piles of multi-coloured carpets to the spot where the dulcimer lay on a lower shelf. It was an antique instrument; its metal strings were meant to be plucked rather than hammered by mallets. At that moment, she noticed an elderly lady emerging from the depths of the store, hobbling towards her.

'You can buy everything in here,' she said to Clara, making a wide, graceful movement with one hand and lowering her glasses with the other to examine her customer.

'The dulcimer,' said Clara. 'Is it still playable?'

'I haven't tried.' The lady chuckled. 'Take your chance.'

They lowered their heads to inspect the instrument more closely. It looked dormant and dreamy, waiting to be played.

'I'll wake you up,' mumbled Clara silently. 'How much?' she asked without altering her bent posture.

With her wrinkled hand, the lady pulled a pen from her pocket and quickly jotted down an amount on a piece of paper. Clara smiled and negotiated the price to less than half. Lifting the dulcimer from its resting place, the shopkeeper blew off some dust from the surface and carried it to the counter, where she clumsily wiped it.

'I have a fine wrapping for that thing,' she proclaimed.

From the storage space underneath a tabletop, she withdrew a reel of packaging paper. It was extraordinary – a vintage print with glowing red stripes, blooming violet-blue orchids, and lemons of bright yellow. Clara's face lit up with delighted surprise.

'My pleasure,' declared the shop lady, handing her the bundle. 'It's as good as new.'

The little bells rang adieu softly as Clara stepped out onto the street, where the dazzling light was competing with cacophonous sounds sweeping the city. Heatwaves swaddled her, and she decided that she couldn't walk too far with that unforeseen load in her arms. She could take a bus to that big shopping mall to rest and refresh herself. The old lady had wound thick red ribbons around the packet with a wooden handle attached to it, and it all seemed to hold well.

While waiting for the bus to arrive, Clara began to caress the glossy paper. Under it, she could feel the smooth wooden panel of the instrument. How devotedly she would polish it and then wind up fresh, bright steel strings to make it shine all over. She would place it on the mantelpiece. On clear days, she would take it into the garden to play it while sitting underneath the canopy of the magnolia tree, where the sounds of the strings being played would be carried away by the gentle breeze passing by.

The scent of the blossoms and the tunes would mingle with the breath of the wind. And the vintage paper … it was far too glamourous and rare to be discarded. She would set it gently and carefully under the pane of a golden picture frame and maybe place it …

The bus screeched piercingly, stopping abruptly in front of Clara. People dashed out from the shiny vehicle like a waterfall, and she hastily climbed aboard. The coolness of the air conditioning was soothing, and an empty seat was right there. She sat down and placed the dulcimer on her lap. From her handbag, she took out the papers for her appointment. There was a map of the area, an invitation letter, and a sheet with her own notes. Time enough to have a drink at the mall and use the lavatory to freshen her neck and hands. In front of her sat two children: a boy and a girl. They wore colourful sleeveless shirts, and Clara began to stare at their bony shoulders. They talked quietly with each other, but for the most part, they were busy working their chewing gums, once in a while blowing them up to pink bubbles of a considerable size, just to let them pop. Suddenly, the girl turned and studied Clara. Then, her eyes wandered to the package on her lap.

'Hey, ma'am. What's that you have inside that flashy paper bag?'

The boy turned his head too.

Clara brushed a strand of hair from her forehead.

'It's a musical instrument,' she smiled.

'Can we see it?' asked the boy.

The girl now knelt on her seat. 'Yeah, what is it?'

She blew another bubble and let it pop pompously as she leaned forward, her reddish hair dangling down, just about touching Clara's knees. Then, suddenly, her hand was fumbling with the glossy paper. Clara gently but firmly shoved the girl's hand back. The children giggled. Now, the boy tried to touch the parcel.

'Stop it,' said Clara.

The girl laughed and pulled at the loose end of the paper, so it began to rip open slightly. Clara's face flushed with angry irritation.

The children giggled away and tried to tear it apart even more. At that moment, the bus stopped, and Clara forcefully pulled herself out of her seat. Clasping her handbag and package, she stumbled out onto the sidewalk. As the bus pulled off, she saw the children laughing behind the window and making faces at her. Her heart was beating wildly. She was overwhelmed by a swirling dizziness in her head and the trembling of her knees. Where was she? The direction was still right, but she was nowhere near the area of her appointment. She found herself in front of another immense shopping centre. With a heavy sigh escaping her, she decided to take a break right there.

Entering the lofty building, she discovered a small café on the ground floor. The only vacant seat she could spot was next to a man sitting at an empty table. He had short legs, a stout neck above a squarely built torso, and a slightly bulging belly. He wore flip-flops and a faded black-and-white striped T-shirt with patches of sweat.

'May I?' she asked.

He nodded slightly while his ebony eyes curiously watched Clara take a seat. She didn't feel very comfortable being that close to him, but she knew she desperately needed to sit down. Having ordered her drink, she noticed the man studying her, just like the children had on the bus. Hastily, she took small sips of the chilly liquid that had been put down in front of her by a weary waitress. The glass was misted up, and the pieces of crushed ice and peppermint leaves moved slowly in a circle after being stirred. The man leaned towards her.

'Everything all right?' he asked, revealing a slight accent.

'Yes, yes,' she replied.

She wished the man would leave her alone. She didn't like him and wondered why he was so impertinent. Clara put down the small straw hat she had been wearing since morning, smoothed out her moss green linen skirt, and pulled down the sleeves of her immaculate white blouse. Her silver bracelets dangled softly as she opened her handbag to check the invitation letter again. There was still time, and she could relax and wind down here for a while.

When she closed her eyes for a moment, she heard him say, 'You're in the wrong part of town.'

Clara straightened herself up with trepidation.

'Well, ma'am. I just saw the letterhead of that paper. And in case you're heading there …'

Fear welled up inside her. She had to wait a long time for this consultation and would be charged if she missed it. Looking at her wristwatch without actually recognising the position of its hands, she began to feel confused and frightened. The city was monstrous and the density of traffic nearly intimidating. Tears appeared in her eyes, and the letter in front of her became blurry. She heard the chair next to her being pushed away and the man ask if he could help. If only he would leave her alone. A tear rolled down her cheek, and she felt ashamed. Clara fingered the parcel, trying to take hold of the dulcimer's strings. The man did not seem to notice that. Eyeing her sharply, he sat down next to her, while he pulled the paper slowly from her damp hand.

'Look,' he said. 'You will have to take the urban railway right away to get there on time. But even then, you probably won't make it.'

Clara wiped her chin as she stood up. Reeling slightly, she asked him about the nearest station. She managed to stash everything back into her handbag and then grasped her hat and the handle of her parcel. A few strips of paper dangled loose, with orchids and lemons now becoming alive, as they fluttered cheerfully in the stream of air that flowed from the large fan in one corner of the café.

'I have to go there myself anyway,' he said.

'Can I carry this for you?'

'No,' said Clara.

Outside, the air seemed muggier than before, and she suddenly couldn't remember exactly what this examination was for. There had been many check-ups lately, and one seemed to have led to another without any clear results. The man was short and had to tilt his head back slightly as he walked directly beside Clara to meet her eyes.

If only he wasn't wearing flip-flops but taller shoes, she thought, while he gently led her to the front of the station, which came into view. And then, she felt a warmth radiating towards her, a loving tenderness, and a feeling of care she hadn't encountered in a long time. With a crowd bustling around them, she felt faint again and cautiously let her arm slide into his. Hesitantly, he patted her slender hand.

Arriving at the large entrance that would swallow her in a moment, he said, 'I think you will make it. Good luck.'

When he smiled at her, his ruddy cheeks lifted up so high that they almost closed his eyes. Her heart was dancing tenderly for a moment.

'Will you tell me what's in this package? Before you go?'

'Oh,' she said, 'it's an old, dusty musical instrument with rusted broken strings that cannot be played. But I will make it glisten and shine and then bring forth celestial sounds that you have never heard before.'

CAPTURED WATER

Back at the café, José found the beer he had ordered with all the froth gone, the rocket salad topping an avocado sandwich wilting, and the pile of fried potatoes viscous and cold. He took the toolbox from his chair, which he had left for the waitress as a sign that he would return. Two more swimming pools in suburbia were waiting for him to clean and maintain today. Captured water always turned turbid while forgivingly gathering fallen leaves and insects that had drifted from their paths. His maintenance work was easier to manage after sunset; only then, he was pestered by the pungent plumes of smoke from various barbecues.

What a peculiar woman that was. Everything about her was pale. Her light blue eyes, her skin and lips, her hair a modestly fair, almost non-existent colour. There was something mystical about her that he could not identify, like an inner strength and decisiveness that tried to permeate through some vague afflictions that seemed to trouble her. It was just that he couldn't bear people being lost and helpless. At the station, he had waited for her to give him her name, at least, though she doubtlessly had been too unsettled and confused to think of it.

José gulped down the stale beer and chewed hastily on some potato slices while he wrapped up the sandwich to tuck away in the pocket of his work trousers. Had she not talked about playing for him on her obscure musical instrument? At that point, she suddenly had a different air about her, radiating confidence and joy. Though he had instantly grasped the date and time of her examination appointment, written in bold type on the invitation letter, he had failed to catch her address. Why was he always trying to act as correctly as he could? José slung the heavy toolbox over one shoulder and paid for both her bill and his own.

It was nearly impossible to meet her again, though he imagined that she most likely lived on the outskirts of the city. She was hardly a swimming pool owner or a barbecue lover. He envisioned her with some cats and lots of books – and he never read any.

THERE ONCE WAS WILDERNESS

'Here comes Daddy,' muttered Henry.

Mimi swiftly flipped her hair back into a ponytail and squinted down the park promenade. Whenever the children spotted Arthur arriving to pick them up, he would bend his knees and do a Groucho Marx walk while beaming at them.

'Why does Daddy do that Groucho thing? And I don't want a rowboat trip,' said Henry. 'Let's go to the museum.'

'Which?' asked Mimi. 'The one with the dioramas?'

'Yep,' said Henry, sliding down from the park bench.

'But we'll have some ice cream first,' added Mimi quickly.

'Daddy, we want ice cream! Lots!' they hollered.

Arthur put his briefcase down, dabbed the sweat from his face, and tousled Henry's shock of hair.

'And it's too hot today for rowing in the pond. Let's do the museum,' said Henry.

Mimi grabbed her father's hand and began to pull him down the gravel path towards the ice cream parlour. The shadows of the trees and bushes had already grown to gigantic lengths, announcing the nearing sunset.

Arthur glanced at Mimi's small back. He sometimes wondered why his children were so skinny. They seemed to eat all the time.

'Cup or cone?' asked the friendly girl.

She wore a pistachio-coloured uniform with a matching cap and glossy lipstick and looked perfectly fresh, despite the heatwave. The glinting balls of ice cream began to seep and run down the crispy waffle cones within seconds, and some dripped to the ground.

'We met a funny woman on the bus today, Daddy.'

Mimi watched her father, who was trying to keep his shirt clear of the ice cream funnels.

'So, what was funny about her?' asked Arthur.

'She carried a fancy-looking packet and said there was a musical instrument inside. But it was all flat. Maybe it was a large book or a chopping board. She wouldn't show it to us.'

'We made fun of her.'

'Why?' asked Arthur.

'She wasn't angry. I mean, at us,' added Henry quickly. 'But she mumbled something strange about the thing in her package as she got off the bus. Something about a dull sea mare.'

'A dull shearer?' repeated Arthur.

'No. A dull sea mare!' cried Mimi, whose cheeks were painted with chocolate sepia and watermelon hues.

Arthur asked himself how he would fix that.

The museum's reception hall was of solemn and majestic splendour. The children began to whisper, and Arthur told them to clean their hands and faces in the basement lavatory. He shoved three of the free admission vouchers he had received at his workplace on the occasion of his birthday last month at the young man at the counter. Checking his watch, he saw that they had just over an hour before closing time.

Henry loved the grandeur of the diorama wing. He always wanted to crawl right onto the platforms and vanish into the expanse of the three-dimensional scenery. Everything on display was frozen in time forever. There was no ageing, decay, or death. Wild animals roamed among the bushy greenery; even birds were forever in flight. Snuggling up with the towering grizzly bear would be perfectly safe, and he wondered if the animal's fur still reeked of wilderness and danger. He could place his cheek carefully upon that massive fuzzy belly and forget about everything for a moment.

'Daddy, when will Mummy be back home?' whispered Mimi.

'Likely in a few weeks,' said Arthur.

'If she still has that plaster on her leg, I'll draw flowers and butterflies on it,' she mused, while Henry pressed his face on the glass panel that separated him from the motionless wilderness and almost forgot about the world.

MYTHS OF LAND AND SEA

Henry looked up and studied the patterns of the fluorescent stars arranged on the ceiling above his bed. He still saw the grizzly with its burdensome head towering above him. Its stiff hind legs were firmly planted on the ground. Its fur was of a dulled colour. It would never see the sunlight again.

Turning on his flashlight, he fumbled for the pen and notebook he kept under his mattress. His mother deserved a welcome back for her day of coming home.

And Henry wrote …

For my Mum!

THE DULL SEA MARE

In ancient times, which were a long time ago, many different animals lived on the earth. Some that now live on land used to live in the ocean. And some that lived in the ocean are now found on land. It was like that.

The fish wanted to see what was outside the water, and others wanted to know what was inside the deep blue sea.

This is also true for horses. One day, a mare said, 'Today's the day!' And she galloped to the beach. She jumped, and because horses are heavy, she drowned right away. But she survived and lived in the sea. It's just that she became dull because algae and other small sea animals began living in her fur.

Then, she had many babies. By and by, all the sea horses became much smaller because it allowed them to swim much better. And they decided to swim standing up. Why not? All their fur was gone. They didn't like the algae.

That's why today we have sea horses.

It's all thanks to the ancient dull sea mare.

Dear Mum, it's great that you are back home and I can help make breakfast again.

I hope you like my story.

I love you,
Henry

He knew she would love it.

A LITTLE SOMETHING

Many leaves had gathered inside the empty swimming pool. The blazing yellow, red, and orange hues set upon the pool's blue paint were such a sight. Sarah couldn't resist the striking view. Hesitantly, she returned to her laptop and tried to focus on the monthly column she would have to submit by tomorrow. It still needed some polishing. She had toyed with the idea of integrating Henry's *The Dull Sea Mare* story, but in the end, it seemed too private. It had been such a personal gift. But she also liked the thought that her son would be published at nearly ten. Sarah couldn't help but smile at that. She kept a few copies of the handwritten original in the drawer of her writing desk and planned to present some to a select number of friends and family members. Her brother definitely had to see it when he came for dinner tonight. Sarah picked up her camera to take a few photos of the festival of colours inside the pool. It would all be removed and gone this afternoon.

Eventually, José found himself wading through heaps of leaves into the depths of the small pool. Why hadn't they covered it in good time? It was such trouble to climb up and down the small ladder time and again, with bulging bags weighing down his back. *I might lose some weight, at least,* he thought. But he knew he wouldn't.

Sarah wrapped a substantial shawl around her shoulders as she bashfully approached the pool ladder. Then, she smiled down at him.

She sure feels guilty for having forgotten to fix the cover in time, José mused.

'Something wrong with your leg?' he asked.

'I tripped, and I toppled.'

'How poetically put.'

'Well, I'm a writer.'

'You are?'

'Only for the local paper. Now and then.'

'I actually like poetry,' he said.

'You do? What kind?'

'Only short poems like yours.' He smiled.

'I simply adore those leaves. Aren't they gorgeous? It's such a shame we have to dispose of them.' Sarah sighed. 'So sorry you have extra work this time. But I have a little something here for you.'

She waved a pale blue envelope in her right hand.

'By the way,' she said, 'my brother's secretary, Mrs Andrew, should have her garden fountain fixed. It's all clogged up with leaves. She lives away from here, though. I tucked her address and phone number under your toolbox on the lawn. She would appreciate it if you called first.'

'Sure thing,' he said, letting the envelope slip into the pocket of his greasy work trousers.

LUCKY I HAD UNDERWEAR

When, some days later, José arrived in front of Mrs Andrew's home, he immediately spotted the garden fountain. It was a rather artistic piece, certainly two hundred years old. She waited for him in front of her porch.

'Mr José?' She waved at him.

'I have some coffee for you. And homemade pumpkin pie with cream. And apple sauce, still warm.'

'Great, ma'am, but later. Let me first have a look at your fountain,' he called back. 'That's why I have this belly fat I can't get rid of,' he muttered. All those cakes, pies, and mounds of whipped cream.

What a bright day it was. The sun set the huge trees, still bearing some of the coloured autumn foliage, aflame. A cold wind made it dance and sparkle. He bent over the basin to inspect the leaves that had clogged it. They were sluggish and brownish, almost having built up to a clumpy, slippery mass. Two tiny spiders scurried in different directions to escape their invaded abode. As he tried to put on the work gloves he took out of his toolbox, a tawny dog came out of nowhere, panting towards him and leaping stormily up his legs. José heard the sound of fabric tearing. He cried out in shock and pain. Puzzled, the dog gaped at him for a moment, only to dash off into the shadows underneath the trees at the far side of the garden. José threw his gloves to the ground and saw Mrs Andrew running towards him.

'So sorry! This is the neighbour's rascal,' she whined.

They looked down at his legs and saw blood beginning to seep quickly into the fabric.

'So sorry, Mr José,' she wailed as she grabbed him by his work jacket and began to pull and push him inside her house.

'Here's the bathroom. And please take off your work clothes; we'll disinfect the scratches.'

She opened and closed the doors of her bathroom cabinet. 'And here! I have enough bandages to stop the bleeding.'

Next, José found himself sitting in his underpants on a dashing living room sofa with a generous slice of pumpkin pie, decorated with freshly whipped cream, and a mug of steaming coffee set on the table before him. Mrs Andrew handed him a big fluffy towel to cover his hairy legs.

'I'll call the neighbour. She certainly will compensate you for the trousers,' she affirmed.

'No need,' replied José faintly. 'They're worn out and should be replaced anyway.'

'No, no. Let me fetch her. And let me know if you need anything else,' replied Mrs Andrew as she briskly left the room.

If he had the coffee now, he wouldn't be able to fall asleep until past midnight. José put the folded towel on his lap for a napkin. While he shoved big chunks of pumpkin pie into his dry mouth, he listened to her muffled voice making a phone call in the other room. And then, someone arrived in the entrance hall, and he heard a dog panting.

'Not again,' he groaned. 'My bare legs!'

The door opened, and his eyes widened.

'Hi, I'm so sorry! My dog escaped and slipped through a hole underneath the fence that we were never able to detect. No worries; he's now waiting in the hall wearing a leash. He just seemed to like you, and …'

Clara froze and removed her sunglasses. As she put her hand to her mouth, her eyes became misty.

Mrs Andrew began to look irritated. 'Do you know each other?'

José stood up, forgetting about his underwear as the towel dropped to the floor.

'His trousers are badly ripped,' said Mrs Andrew.

Clara took a deep breath.

'Definitely. I'll fix the trousers.'

INTO ABYSMAL DEPTHS

Standing inside her living room, Clara and José looked at each other in silence. She made a gesture, and once more, he sat down on an ornate couch, wearing only his underpants while holding the bundle of his dirty clothes tightly in his arms.

'I'll get you a plaid,' said Clara. 'Can I offer you a drink? How in the world could this happen? To meet again?' She shook her head in disbelief.

Clara left for the kitchen, and the dog had cuddled himself up on a plush bed near the masonry fireplace, where a small ember was crackling. He was quietly chewing and licking a toy. Large windows provided a view of a lovely garden with wild autumn flowers and a single majestic magnolia tree. By now, grey clouds had moved in and the tearing of the wind made some of the remaining leaves, still clinging to the twigs, swirl and sail to the ground. In a small niche of the room was a chest of drawers topped by an empty vase. Above it hung a large golden frame with a captivating picture, and José suddenly recognised the package paper with its violet-blue blossoming orchids and yellow lemons on red stripes.

'You feeling better?' he asked when she came back, handing him a woollen plaid and a large glass of soda with freshly cut chunks of lime.

'I'm perfectly fine,' she smiled at him. 'And really always was. Please give me your pants. I'll fix them so you can drive back home, at least. It has become quite chilly outside today.'

Clara unrolled the bundle and uttered, 'And look at those large rips! Oh, there seem to be some heavy tools in your pockets. You'll have to empty them first.'

'Where shall I put them?' he asked. 'They're dirty.'

She took a paper napkin with a pastel floral print from one of the drawers and spread it on the coffee table. One by one, the tools and then the blue envelope emerged. It was crinkled and a little soiled.

'I have a sewing machine,' said Clara. 'It will only take me a few minutes.'

It had become darker in the room, and José stretched to switch on the table lamp beside him. Then, he saw the first snowflakes of the season floating in the air outside. He began to sip the sweet and sour drink while listening to the sound of her sewing machine. It was somewhat soothing, and he noticed that he began to relax. The pulsating pain from the scratches had almost subsided by now, and the bandages were wrapped tightly and skillfully. The dog had fallen asleep. Whimpering, he moved his paws slightly while dreaming.

José stared at the items on the table in front of him, and then, he reached out to open the envelope. He unfolded a piece of paper with the clumsy handwriting of a child. When Clara returned, she found José laughing silently.

'What happened?' she asked. 'I know. The way we met again is remarkable. I'm just as confused as you are.'

'Look at this,' he said. 'A client of mine gave it to me the other day. It must be by one of her kids.'

She put down the stitched trousers on a chair next to José, whose belly still shook as he chuckled. Clara's eyes ran over the lines, and her face lit up. She smiled.

'Children!' she said. 'What a pity we adults have lost the gift of a free and wild imagination. We rarely ever have our heads in the clouds or dive into the depths of an abyss as deep as the ocean, like this youngster.' She returned the crumpled sheet to José, who scrambled to put it back into the envelope.

'You can keep it. If you like,' he said.

'No, it was given to you. But I'll never forget it. It's so peculiar: *The Dull Sea Mare.*'

'Didn't you want to play your musical instrument for me?' asked José.

'Right!' she said. 'The dulcimer. I'll get it.'

He arranged the plaid around him and saw her remove a beautiful piece of cloth to reveal a wooden board that leaned upon the mantelpiece. Its varnished surface reflected the lights inside the room, and the metal wire strings glinted fresh and new. Clara sat down close to him and placed the instrument solemnly on her lap. Waiting for a moment, she let her fingers hover gracefully above the strings. She smiled a little.

And then, she began to play …

About the Stories

The opening story to this collection of five short stories, *Radiant Jewels*, was first written in 2005. This was followed by *Mountain Creatures* in 2011, *The Dull Sea Mare* in 2021, *Five Stars* in 2022, and *Akashic Records* in 2023.

The era of the Eastern European shtetl and its inhabitants has long vanished. But their descendants can still be found all over the world. As a fantasy piece, *Radiant Jewels* touches on the ancestry of a much acclaimed and famed singer-songwriter, who is also known for his electric blue eyes.

Some other world-famous individuals, James Joyce, Vladimir Uljanov, later known as Lenin, and Hermann Hesse were all staying in Switzerland at the end of World War I. In *Mountain Creatures*, they meet at Monte Verità, a local vegetarian community, known for its intrepid health regime. While, in real life, the actual Joyce was usually undaunted and acted confidently, in this story, he finally meets his master. Thus, slightly insecure and intimidated, he has to find his way about the given circumstances. As for Hesse here, he *had* visited his place of longing, India, which he in fact bypassed on his journey to East Asia.

Leaving southernly regions behind, the high mountain settings that inspired *Five Stars* recently experienced a lack of snowfall in the depths of winter. Hills and mountains, once covered with a thick layer of snow, are now brownish green. Prestigious hotels were demolished and replaced with stylish wellness resorts. Mere tourism has turned into a mass phenomenon, and nature has to yield and withdraw. It is time for some nostalgia.

It's not a big step from remembering the charms of the past to delving into deeper and more mystical aspects of life. As in *Akashic Records*, extraordinary coincidences and unexpected twists and turns sometimes do happen. They seem to be part of the mysteries of life. In this story, it is possible to visit beautiful places in the world, even though they are increasingly flooded with visitors, and it seems that sometimes, sudden changes of course are required so that new perspectives can take shape.

The closing story in this book, *The Dull Sea Mare*, is a commentary on several essential themes. How can personal setbacks and trials be overcome? How can we cope with hectic urban lifestyle and other demands of modern living? How might we soften our prejudices towards others for a closer mutual understanding? How to find our true passions and talents? Despite whatever challenges may arise, there are ways to discover good things happening in life and to eventually realise individual fulfilment.

About the Author

While skilled as a visual artist,
Marion Sommer's joy in creating images
through words has always prevailed.
She has also been fond of reading
compellingly written short stories, and
this collection is her first publication
in this category. Other works are the
illustrated *Ornamental Cats* and
The Dull Sea Mare, both printed
in colour as unique gift books, and
the children's book *Milson.*